# The Winter Wardens

By Erica Leduc

The Winter Wardens by Erica Leduc



Illustrations by Višnja Mihatov Barić

Published by Lilac Arch Press Saskatchewan, Canada
www.lilacarchpress.com

For Deanna Casey,
and all those that loved her

# Table of Contents

Glossary of Terms

Fae—Creatures that are fairies. They look like humans and are typically the same height as humans.

Rechkin—A creature that is of the Winter Fae realm. They have antlers like an elk, the body of a bear, and long shaggy fur.

Wyvern—A small dragon-like fae creature that has two legs.

<u>**Chapter One**</u>

The storm was expected, but it wasn't supposed to be this bad. It certainly wasn't supposed to snow. It was also a few days early.

Elizabeth blinked through the snow as the fog rose around her. Her boat rocking through the harsh waters.

What was supposed to be an easy trip to do her seasonal check of the hazard buoys had become dangerous. Her dog, Sable sat hunched by Elizabeth's feet in the little fishing boat.

Elizabeth patted her. Why hadn't she taken Neil Lewis's kid up on the offer to do the check for her? Right. Because they were her responsibility, and she could do it fine.

Her family had been maintaining the buoys for a hundred and twenty-five years. Ever since her great great great grandfather had built the house. Her house, now. It was her responsibility.

Into the fog, she saw one of the buoys flashing through the storm. She had to get more to the west if she wanted to get back to shore. She had to go against the waves.

Maybe she was too old for this.

Everyone had been trying to tell her that, but without saying it. But, seventy-three didn't feel old. She was still healthy and fit. Her friend Violet said it was all the fresh ocean air that kept Elizabeth so healthy. What Violet didn't know is that Elizabeth wasn't in the peak of health.

Physically she was all right. She had some bronchitis, a blood clot disorder to keep an eye on, and some days her body didn't want to go as fast as she would like it to.

But what weighed on her was that she knew some things were going on with her memory. She would forget a name or a word, and it would be on the tip of her tongue, but she wouldn't be able to remember it. Yet, she knew that she should know it. That she did know it.

There were other things too. She would make something for dinner. Later she would realize  that she already had made that, and there was some of that same dish sitting in the fridge. She knew she ought to talk to Doctor Dabrysiak about it. She would, soon. Just in case.

She felt the impact come up the bottom of the boat before she heard the jagged sound of the hull hitting rocks.

The choppy waters had made the impact harsh, throwing Sable and Elizabeth both off balance. Cold seeped into every inch of her that had landed on the bottom of the boat. Sable scrambled to get her footing. Water was splashing. Another wave came on, throwing the little boat into the rocks harder this time.

Elizabeth pulled herself up to the seat as she felt the water rushing in. She tried to see through the wet, heavy snow and the fog. It was settling onto the boat, on her, and on Sable's fur.

Where the snow met the warmth of Elizabeth or Sable, it melted rather quickly. But it wasn't melting as fast when it hit the boat. Not a good sign.

The worsening cold was becoming more and more of a risk factor, especially with the decreasing daylight.

There!

Rocky cliff faces jutted up. She scanned to each side, following the looming shape of the cliffs.

It wasn't just a few rocks. She looked for familiar landmarks, hoping to see a sign of the old lighthouse or a glimpse of somebody's dock. A small alcove set into the cliffs. It was still rocky, but she liked the odds of getting herself there.

"Let's take our chances," she told Sable.

She should be able to figure out where exactly she was once she got into the land a bit. Find Coastal Street and walk that back to the town if she had to. She used one of the emergency oars to push them off the rocks and get the boat aligned towards the alcove. Battling against the waves she steered the boat towards the bay, getting the waves to work with her.

They took on more water. Rocks in the shallow water scraped the hull. She got out of the boat, guiding it to the shore and pulling it onto the rocks there. Sable hopped out.

The damage to the boat was bad enough that the small patch kit she had wouldn't be enough. It would need a proper repair before she could take it out again. She secured the boat as best she could. Coastal Street should be a thirty-minute walk.

"Come on, let's go," she said. It was a steep walk up. She felt it throughout her body and she wanted to stop more than once. But, if she stopped, she wasn't sure she would start going again. She was tiring and wanted nothing more than to lay down. Even right there for only a few moments. But that would be deadly.

What felt like hours later, she got to levelled out ground. It wasn't an area she recognized at all. The rocky oceanside gave way to the forest. Either way, Coastal Street should be close enough, if she was in the right place. How far from her course had she strayed?

She trudged through the thickening slush, breaking off a few twigs here and there. Keep a trail, she thought.

The clouds had darkened the sky, heavy with snow. It was getting darker and darker by the minute. She needed to at least find shelter. That's it, she decided, if she wasn't on the road soon, she would stop and make a shelter.

There was something about this weather that felt...wrong. September was too early for snow, and the storm had come out of what seemed like nowhere. The forecast had called for heavy rain a few days out and coming from the southeast. But this had come from the north, sudden and fast. Still, no road.

She would go a bit further. Sable's ears shifted to the right. All four legs tensed, her neck elongated and stiff, her tail straight out and high. She was listening. Elizabeth paused and listened also. The creak of trees, the onslaught of wind, everything sodden with heavy wet snow.

"Let's go," Elizabeth commanded. If there was something out there, better to keep moving and try to get to the road.

As they went, she was sure that what Sable was so intent on, wasn't just the dog's imagination. What would be out in this? Most creatures this time of year would be taking shelter. There weren't many predators in this area, a few coyotes mostly.

If it was a moose, they would be in trouble. Elizabeth had crossed paths with a moose once and didn't need to have another encounter to know how dangerous they could be. Sable kept looking to the right.

With a feeling of suddenness, the forest thinned out. She could see a small valley, with an inlet back to the ocean. There was a small house with lights on in the front half. Smoke came up from the chimney. A house should mean the road. She couldn't see it from where she was, but it shouldn't be far from the house.

Sable snarled to their right. Then, warning barks echoed. Elizabeth stopped and turned, looking through the trees. But, it was closer than that. The body of a creature. But, not any she could identify. It was immense. Triple the size of a car. It had long shaggy fur and thick antlers. It almost had a face that resembled a cat, but with a hardened rock covering the forehead.

"Get away from it! Hurry!" A man's voice shouted to her from the house.

She jumped and scrambled through the snow towards the home. As she got to the space that had been cleared for the house, she felt a vibration rise around her. It felt as though it went through her, rattling her jaw.

# Chapter 1 Discussion Questions

1. What is your favorite weather?

_______________________________

2. Share, think or write about a time you were caught in bad weather.

_______________________________

_______________________________

3. Share any experiences you have had in boats.

_______________________________

_______________________________

_______________________________

4. Have you ever been/or felt lost?

_______________________________

_______________________________

_______________________________

5. Have you had a pet you loved?

_______________________________

_______________________________

# Chapter 2

"What on earth?" Elizabeth panted as she reached the porch.

"Do not stop. You need to get inside, make sure your dog goes with you," the man directed. He eased the door open more for her to get through.

"Sable," Elizabeth whispered, beckoning to her. The dog didn't budge at first.

"Sable," Elizabeth urged, halfway through the door. Sable came to her, quickly turning back the way they had come.

"Come on, in, let's go." She nudged Sable the rest of the way inside.

Elizabeth went in. They were in a kitchen, she went to the window. She could just make out the bulk of the creature from the window.

"What was that?" she asked.

"It's a rechkin," he explained, "It's on the other side of the ward, don't worry, it won't infect us here."

"Infect us? A ward?" she asked, confused and concerned.

"Almost like a shield. You can't see it? Shimmering a bit green all around the house?"

Elizabeth looked at the sky, then at the snow on the ground. Other than the creature, everything looked normal to her. Not a hint of green shimmer.

"No"

He frowned a bit but kept looking out the window. As the silence stretched, the creature paced. Elizabeth had never seen anything like it.

"It was sick. It shouldn't be here at all. We'll have to wait." he told her, glancing her way before looking intently out the window.

"Just a little bit. Is there any way to get rid of it? You said it wasn't supposed to be here, where is it from?"

"Another world, if you'd believe it."

Looking at the creature, she more than believed it. The brown shaggy fur seemed to almost reflect the light from the house back at them.

"Thank you for helping us," she told him.

"You're welcome, I think you'd best stay the night. I've got a spare room for you and your dog. How'd you get here in the first place?"

"Caught in the storm, I was blown off course. Could you take me into town? I can pay you. Or if you can't I'll call a taxi or something." She looked around the cabin for a phone that she could use

.

"Town? There's no town here." He told her, "We're not on the mainland, this is an island about six miles off the mainland."

Okay. She could figure this out. She would….

Actually, what would she do? She looked at Sable, who was growling at the window softly. She would be staying the night then, tomorrow she could see about repairing the boat and getting home.

"All right then, I guess I'll be taking you up on that offer," she told him, looking at the cabin. It was small but furnished comfortably and well.

"I'm Elizabeth, and this is Sable," she introduced.

"My name is Alant. It's a pleasure to meet you, despite the circumstances."

As the darkness grew, a dark blue and purple mist rose from the creature. Elizabeth watched as it disappeared.

The mist blanketed the forest floor. It rolled towards them, but stopped suddenly, as though a glass wall was in the way. It climbed up, and over the house.

"The ward," Alant said, watching it also. Slowly, the mist cleared and they were left with just the falling snow. The ordeal seeming over. He pointed out the bathroom and the spare room to her before he made them tomato soup and cheese sandwiches. Sable got some as well since he didn't have any dog food.

They were sitting at the kitchen table, next to a pile of books. There was some paper with scribbles on it she couldn't make out, and some pencils scattered throughout it all.

"So, the what did you call it? A rechkin?"

He nodded, chewing on the sandwich.

"It's sick you said, what is it sick with? Is there a way to cure it?"

"As far as I know there isn't a way to cure the creature itself."

Well, that wasn't good. Sick animals were prone to doing things outside of their normal behaviour. She wasn't interested in seeing what else this one might do.

"What is a rechkin, exactly? It looks like a bear and an elk dressed in a woolly mammoth coat."

He laughed at that. "You know, that's not a bad way of putting it." He put his sandwich aside and flipped over one of the papers with writing on it.

"Say we're here," he drew a small horizontal line across the paper, then tapped above the line. "The rechkin, and others like it, come from here," he tapped below the line.

"This 'here' below the line is," he paused, "A bit like another world. It's part of our world but sort of hidden behind a veil. It's not very often that it happens that something comes through. But, every so often it does."

He explained further. "And this one was sick. If that mist had touched us, or any living creature with a heartbeat, it would have infected us within 12 hours."

She looked out the window. She needed to get home. Whatever this all was, it was weird. Weird and not anything she could understand. She looked to Sable, who was watching them as they ate. She would deal with getting home tomorrow.

Chapter 2 Discussion Questions

1. Has  there been a time in your life that you have met a kind stranger?

______________________________

______________________________

2. Have you ever seen a creature and felt unsure what it was?

______________________________

______________________________

3. Do you have a favourite type of sandwich? What toppings do you like/dislike?

______________________________

______________________________

4. A rechkin sounds like a bizarre creature. Using your imagination invent your own strange creature.

______________________________

______________________________

## Chapter 3

Elizabeth woke up the next day to an even worse storm than the night before. Hail and sleet battered at the small bedroom window. She could smell coffee. She went to the kitchen, with Alant nowhere in sight. She helped herself to some coffee. Then she slid her coat on and went to the porch. In the light of day, the events of last night seemed somehow muted. They were still present though.

Her morning slipped into the afternoon when Alant finally returned from fixing a fence. The afternoon faded into evening, and the storm raged on.

A week later the wind still had not let up, and the snow had not stopped.

Their days took on a routine. They'd have coffee in the morning, then she would go out with him and look for signs of the sickness. They'd have a quick bite to eat. Later they'd drive the old buck and rail fence-line. They checked for spots that needed repair, and repaired them as needed.

The wind, snow, and ice were bitterly cold and relentless one day. It was late afternoon when they came back to the cabin and a woman was standing before the house.

She had light red hair that shimmered into blonde, and eyes that seemed almost empty. She said nothing to Elizabeth, but stared at Alant.

Alant stopped a few feet from her.

She just stared, vacant eyes looking at Alant. Her mouth twitched into a smirk that made Elizabeth's stomach curdle.

"There have been many deaths. This needs to be fixed." she said, her words coming out in a hum that could have been pleasant had it not felt like ice piercing her ears.

"Reis?" Alant asked.

"Safe. This is your job, Warden. You need to correct this. Do it, or I will. If you ever want to see Reis again, make it happen." she threatened.

"I'll handle it." he said, equally as hostile.

She turned and left, disappearing into the woods. Before Elizabeth could say anything, Alant huffed off in the opposite direction.

Elizabeth was left alone with her thoughts, and Sable.

Alant came back a few hours after the woman had come and gone. He was still quiet and withdrawn, but she could sense that the walk had done him some good. He went down the stairs to prepare for the evening's fire.

"What do you think, hmm?" she asked Sable, knowing she wouldn't get an answer. "It feels like there's something I'm supposed to be doing but I can't remember what it is."

Sable opened her eyes, looking up from her blanket on the floor. She wagged her tail.

"What's going on here, and who is that woman that came here?" Elizabeth asked no one in-particular.

"She's a long story," Alant answered, coming up from the basement.

Elizabeth turned.

"I have some journals you should read," he told her, seeming unsure, "It might not answer all of your questions, but they will answer some of them, and probably better than I can."

Would she get the answers she wanted though? Probably not, and yet she needed to know. Was she involved? Was this feeling of being connected to everything, and connected to Alant, some sort of bad reaction to being stranded and unable to get home?

"Do you and I," she trailed of for a moment, "Do we know each other?" she asked, not expecting him to answer.

"Yes, but it's," he hesitated, as though he was looking for the right thing to say, "I know you have questions about the past few days. There's a reason that the storm happened and brought you here. I'll be honest I don't know exactly what caused the storm. All I know is something is off where we come from."

"What do you mean, where we come from? I'm from here," Elizabeth said.

Alant started heading for the door, "We're not, and the easiest way is to show you. It's not far."

# Chapter 3 Discussion Questions

1. Have you met someone who was familiar, but you weren't sure why?

_______________________________

_______________________________

2. Have you welcomed unexpected visitors before?

_______________________________

_______________________________

3. Do you prefer coffee, tea, or another hot beverage? How do you take this drink?

_______________________________

4. What would you do if bad weather stranded you in a cabin on an island for a week?

_______________________________

_______________________________

_______________________________

# Chapter 4

Alant got his coat and boots on.

Well, if it wasn't far, Elizabeth supposed she could and should go. She got her outdoor gear on and followed him out. Sable was following closely behind.

He took them into the woods, following what seemed like an old game trail for a bit before he took a turn off the path.

She could only see a bit of the sky through the thickness of the trees. It was a clear winter evening, stars high above them.

"Just here," he told her, stopping. They were in a narrow corridor of trees.

She gasped as it appeared, a large arched doorway with twin doors.

As the doors swung open, she could see a city, cloaked in the night with huge snow-trees behind it. Buildings and towering skyscrapers with pale light in the windows. She took hurried steps towards it.

"Elizabeth!" Alant called out, "You can't!"

She slowed but kept walking. She wanted to see the city itself, to walk the streets that she knew would be cobblestone, to look up at the buildings that she knew would be black marble. A heavy wind rose around them, snow swirling. He grabbed her arm, pulling her to a stop.

"You can't," he told her. He had to shout over the wind, "It's where we are from, not where we belong."

She turned to him.

"We are Wardens of the place, we keep creatures like the rechkin, or worse, from leaving, he explained. "I wanted you to see the lights. You see them, in the buildings?"

She nodded.

"Those lights represent the Winter Wolf, and they're the wrong colour. They are pale, but they should be dark blue. You used to be the best creature healer among the fae. I think that's why the storm blew you to the island, I think the wolf knew that you were its only hope."

"Why don't I remember any of this?" She watched, yearning to hear her footfalls on the snow through the door, to feel the breeze sing through the giant trees as she approached the city.

The doors began to close, the wind died down, and the snow settled.

"It was taken from you," he said, so quietly she could hardly hear it.

"How come?"

"Because you protected something that you believed in. The woman that was here, that's what she wanted. She wanted me to take the past week from you, and wipe your memory again."

He exhaled heavily, and his next words were choked out. "Honestly Elizabeth, had it not been for the weather we've had, I probably would have done it. But, I think that you were brought here right now for a reason."

She wished the door would open again and she could run through it.

Alant said, "We're part of the Winter Court"

He added,"Some would call us fairies, or fae because of our connection to the elements. We help to govern winter, the season, on this plane."

"And my job was to keep creatures there, in Winter?"

He pulled her back towards the way they had come, but she stood not wanting to leave.

"Yes, that was our job. Some creatures would come through and, intentionally or not, leak into and likely destroy the mortal world.

But, we would also heal and help creatures that got injured or trapped here."

The door fully closed. They stood there looking at it for a moment. Did he feel the same pull towards it that she did? She forced herself to turn away.

Potion

Chapter 4 Discussion Questions

1. Is there anything you have had to guard or protect, (perhaps an item, secret, idea, or person)?

________________________________________

________________________________________

2. What places in nature do you enjoy?

________________________________________

________________________________________

3. If you could create a magical world what would it look like?

________________________________________

________________________________________

________________________________________

________________________________________

4. What are some stories you remember that had fairies in them?

________________________________________

________________________________________

# Chapter 5

The next morning Elizabeth sat at the kitchen table with a cup of coffee in her hand.

A stack of leather journals was nearby. She picked one up and began reading, her heart throbbing in her throat. Answers.

*We're finally at our posting. I will miss Winter, though I am glad to have Elizabeth here with me. We are to have a cabin near the gate, and a ward will be put up around us. Our job is to keep everything that would seek to unbalance the seasons in Winter. I know there are some, like Leonora, that would wish to see the mortals gone from this plane and consume it in an eternal frost.*

*But to do so would be the ruin of Winter itself. Part of the power of Winter is that it is fleeting.*

So, it wasn't just creatures that they had to keep from stalking the mortal lands, it was a political movement as well.

*Today we took back a group of young fae that seemed to wander through the gate. It was led by Reis. I wonder if he came here consciously or if he was drawn here by his flesh and blood being on this plane. He cannot know, she wouldn't dare tell him for fear of him coming here intentionally. The danger would be too great, to him, the mortal realm, and all of Winter.*

Reis? Who was that, and what was that about a fae's flesh and blood is there, on the mortal plane? How did that work out?

*Of course, Elizabeth insisted that it was her doing. She claimed that she told the princess to bring it to her.*

*Elizabeth is sentenced to exile, on account of her healing the dragon and defying orders, and trying to influence the royal family.*

*To be in exile means Elizabeth won't know who she is. She will live as a mortal for the rest of her days. She will have no idea of the good she has done, no idea of what or who she is.*

*It will leave me alone to do this work. We are Winter Wardens. Like all wardens of all seasons, we are bonded to each other forever.*

So, she had gone against orders and been banished for it.

It wasn't the answer she had wanted, and it helped explain why she felt so connected to Alant in the first place. But it left her with more questions.

*I saw Elizabeth today, she was near her land she'd been granted, although I think she believes she came to it through a kinship. She was out, attending to warning buoys and beacons connected to her land.*

*She had a dog with her. We always wanted to get one while we were both wardens. I'm pleased she finally got one. It's been so many years since she was exiled.*

*It's been so many years since I've seen anyone but Leonora, who only comes to antagonize me. I wish I could at least see Reis, or talk with Elizabeth and work beside her once more.*

1. Have you kept a diary or a journal? If so, what kinds of things do you write about?

_______________________________

_______________________________

2. Have you ever read someone else's journal?

_______________________________

_______________________________

3. Do you have a favorite city or place to go?

_______________________________

_______________________________

4. Have you ever rescued or cared for an animal in need?

_______________________________

_______________________________

# Chapter 6

Elizabeth glanced at Sable, who was sleeping deeply by the fireplace. Warm light was spilling onto her. She went back to the journals, and as she read into the morning, the frequency of the entries seemed to take on a pattern. Every winter, there were more and more accounts of creatures trying to come through, with them getting smarter and more dangerous each year.

Alant wrote that he thought it may be intentional. Maybe, a fae was sending these creatures on purpose, testing his abilities as a warden, or testing how difficult it would be to break through. The accounts started closer and closer to the beginning of autumn each year, and then further into spring.

He wrote about his intention to meet with the wardens of spring, summer, and autumn to find out if they were experiencing the same thing. But, his contact with the fae world had almost entirely been cut off since she had been banished.

*Looking forward to seeing Reis today. Does he want to see me though? I often wonder, but how do I even start to ask him that?*

*He's taking on such responsibility, the first fae ambassador. Learning not only the rules of our court but also those of autumn and winter also. I wish that Elizabeth could see him; I know she would be proud.*

The door to Alant's room opened and he came through, pulling his blue flannel on over his shirt. She looked up from the journals.

"Thank you, for letting me read these," she told him.

"You're welcome, did it help?" He poured himself some of the coffee.

"In some ways, yes. I have more questions though," she admitted.

He shook the coffee pot, looking at her. She pushed her cup forward. He topped off her mug.

"Who is Reis?" she asked first. He sat down.

"Reis is my son, he's fae." he sighed.

"And his mother?" she asked, worried and unsure if she wanted to know the answer.

"A battle with a wayward wyvern, when Reis was still young."

"Was she a warden also?" Elizabeth asked.

"No," he smiled, "You and she got on well though. She had a farm, just inside the gateway that was attacked by wyverns. She harvested snowberries.

She would come and visit here a few times a month. She and I grew close." He shrugged. "It was a long time ago now," He sipped his coffee and grew quiet.

"And the meeting, with the other wardens, did you ever get that?" she asked quietly.

He looked up at her, frowning. "No. No, I didn't. Why do you ask?"

She went through what she had found, showing him the pattern.

"You see, each year the number of creatures coming through the winter gate increases, as does the number of creatures with illnesses.

You wrote that you believe it's happening for the other courts too. I think we need to find that out, along with healing the Winter Wolf. How do we do that?"


"We would have to go through Reis, and I don't want to put him at odds with Leonora. While she's all about an eternal winter here as well as in our world, fortunately, she does understand that Winter needs the other seasons to truly thrive. The seasons can only happen here. They don't happen anywhere else. But, she's used him against me before, and she'll do it again."

She hesitated. She didn't want to push, and she needed to say this in the best way possible.

"I don't know, I'm not a parent, but maybe it's all right to let Reis decide that for himself now? If he's the one that is in contact with all the seasons, he would be a good person to talk to. Not just for getting the wardens together but also for what is discussed and figured out during that meeting."

He sighed and gave her a sad smile,

"You're probably right." He downed the rest of his coffee. "As for healing the wolf, I've got old logs of yours that might help." He left, going to the basement and came back with a box. He set it at her feet, and then another. He also set down a small, corked bottle.

"I don't know if it will help, but I've been saving this, if you want it. It won't bring all your memories back, but it should help a bit."

She looked at it, she wanted answers, and she also wanted to go back to how things had been. She was content in her life. She didn't need this.

"Thank you," she told him, not touching the bottle.

She took the lid off the first box. Inside were hardcover notebooks, all the same, all neatly organized with dates running along the spine.

She started with the earliest one. It was dated nearly 200 years ago. She opened it and gasped. It was one thing to be told all these things, to sense and feel them, but this was tangible.

Inside was her handwriting. She flipped through the book, all of it in her handwriting. While Alant's had been personal stories, what Elizabeth had done were strictly logs. Each incident or creature that had gone through the gate and been taken back. There were also entries for each creature that had been healed, what had been used and what the outcome had been.

She read well into the night, and as she did, she started to feel as though she knew herself a bit better. She felt like this was something that she had always done and always would do.

As the minutes turned into hours, she found herself wondering if maybe she should drink the tonic Alant had offered.

We helped guide a wounded unicorn back to Winter today. Before we did, I was able to help heal his wound.

Wound:  on the left back leg, about 1 inch long and deep. Seems to have been made by claws.

Treatment: stitched (with Alant's help) and put a mixture of softened and crushed chamomile and lavender over the stitches

Chapter 6 Discussion Questions

1. Do you have any children in your life?

_______________________________

_______________________________

2. If you had lived for the past 200 years, what are some things you would have liked to see?

_______________________________

_______________________________

_______________________________

3. Do you like finding patterns in things?

_______________________________

4. Do you think Elizabeth should drink the tonic? What makes you think this?

_______________________________

_______________________________

_______________________________

# Chapter 7

It took two days of going through her logs and discussing things with Alant. There were two days of getting everything ready in between the day-to-day duties that Alant had to carry out.

Alant had saved some of her old stuff, and she went through her logs. She got herbs together that she could find in the winter, and made small vials of medicines and balms. They finally had a plan, and it was in motion.

Elizabeth and Sable were at the gate, waiting. A white owl perched in one of the trees looked down at them through the snow. Elizabeth felt the tonic in her pocket. Just in case.

The doors started to creak open. She could see three figures coming toward her through the heavy snow. The lights shone in the windows of the city, still pale.

Alant was at the front, talking with a young man who had an ageless quality to him. He had dark tidy hair, and even from there she could see that he had the same eyes as Alant. It had to be Reis.

Next to Reis was a woman who possessed the same agelessness but magnified. She didn't look young though.

She had long frost-white hair that halfway down turned into a blue as deep and dark as the night sky itself. Princess Janara.

The three stepped through the gate, Reis smiled warmly at her.

"Elizabeth, it's incredible to see you," he told her, hugging her close.

Despite the coolness that radiated off him, Elizabeth felt comfortable in the embrace. She had known him, she realized since he was born.

"I'm sorry, I don't remember," she stammered, looking to Alant. There was an immense sense of guilt and confusion rocking around inside of her. She was supposed to know these people.

"It's okay, I know," Reis reassured. "This is Princess Janara," he introduced.

"Nice to meet you again, your highness," Elizabeth said, tilting her head down in a small acknowledgement of Janara's title.

"I brought you this," Janara beamed, holding out her hand and opening it up. There was a beautiful metal bracelet in the palm of her hand. Elizabeth took it and slipped it on. It was warm, and there was a small trembling feeling to it. She noted it was similar to the cluster of bracelets Janara wore.

"Put it on," Janara said.

When she said that, Elizabeth did it, without thinking or being able to stop herself.

"Sorry!" Janara exclaimed. "I need to be more careful with that," she said awkwardly. Elizabeth looked to Alant.

"She's royal, if she makes a command, we're obligated to follow it- whether we want to or not," Alant explained.

"Sorry. But, the bracelet... I enchanted it so that when you go through the gate, it will read you as me. It will only last for five hours though. My abilities are still limited." Janara explained.

"Thank you, Janara, this is amazing." Elizabeth was grateful. This would mean they should be able to get to the wolf and heal it without any interruptions or worry of them.

The group went through the gate. Elizabeth instantly felt as though a weight had been lifted from her. It was also bitter cold. Sable hopped through the snow, her front legs sinking to her shoulders, burying her face in the snow.

They trudged through the snow. Janara knew where the Winter Wolf made their den. While they walked, Janara told Elizabeth what she knew about the Winter Wolf. As old as winter itself, the Winter Wolf would journey to where the moon met the sky and howl through the night.

"Here it is," Janara breathed heavily, exertion from the uphill hike distinct in each word. They were at a small mountain ridge. Janara took them to the base of the mountain, and into a rough cave entrance. Ahead of them, there was a dim glimmer of endless clusters of amethyst.

They had travelled deep into the mountain range when Elizabeth spotted a flash of luminous ashen fur, followed by a low and steady growl. The Winter Wolf stood; teeth bared in a snarl. They all stopped. The wolf stood its ground. Elizabeth took a step forward. The wolf snapped at the air.

She kept trying. She started speaking to the wolf, telling it about what she had done before. She shared that she knew it was sick and she was there to help. Nothing was working. The wolf wasn't leaving but also wasn't letting them approach.

She felt for the tonic in her pocket. This wasn't working.  The bracelet pulsed on her arm. She only had so much time. She took out the tonic.

"What will happen when I drink this?"

"You might get some memories back, or you might not. They will likely be of the wolf or one of us. It's whatever is present with you." Alant answered her.

Okay. She uncorked it and put the cork in her pocket, then drank it. As far as magical potions go, it tasted a bit like cream soda. She expected something closer to cough medicine.

There wasn't anything at first, and then there were some flashes through her mind, memories flooding in. Her and Alant guiding a Pegasus back to winter. Running through the snow with Reis dodging the snowballs he was throwing at her while they laughed.

Janara with tears in her eyes and a baby dragon in her arms. A deep gouge in the Winter Wolf's shoulder had something sinister about it.

She looked at the wolf now. "Do you not remember me either? I helped you before." The wolf growled, less intensely though.

"I am here to help you," Elizabeth begged. Elizabeth slowly got down to the wolf's level, not making eye contact so that the wolf would understand she wasn't a threat. She took the bag off her shoulder and opened it up. She brought out the cloths, tonics, and balms that she had brought.

"Your light is sick, and fae are dying. Winter fae are dying and sick. I need to help you, please."

The wolf took a small step forward. Then another, and another. As it came out from the shadows and crystals, it was obvious what part of the issue was. The Winter Wolf was pregnant, and due soon.

Janara gasped, Reis said something, but Elizabeth didn't catch it. Her focus was on her patient. The wolf sniffed at Elizabeth. She noted that the wolf's breathing was a bit off. The sound coming through her nostrils had contributed to the growling sounds.

Elizabeth got to work, trying to remember all that she had read, to recall memories that she knew she should have.

Chapter 7 Discussion Questions

1. Do you like dogs or do you prefer cats?

_______________________________

_______________________________

2. If you could meet any royalty, real or fictional, who would it be? Why?

_______________________________

_______________________________

3. Have you explored a cave or cavern before?

_______________________________

4. What is your favourite gemstone?

_______________________________

5. Do you prefer silver or gold?

_______________________________

## Chapter 8

She put her hands on the wolf, then her head next to the wolf's lungs. That's where the problem was. There, in the wolf's right lung. A sort of rattle could be heard. Elizabeth exhaled, relieved. She could fix this, and she knew how.

She put together sage, mint, and liquorice root into a small bundle and burned them, coaxing the wolf to sniff and inhale them. Elizabeth turned to Janara.

"Would you be able to come and do this again in a few days, and then a few days later check on how she's doing?"

"Of course, just leave me with what I will need."

Next Elizabeth poured a small bit from one of the vials into her hand and presented it to the wolf, who sniffed it before lapping it up.

Elizabeth set everything down and started slowly putting her things away.

As she wrapped some of the vials, the wolf began to breathe a bit easier.Then, the ragged sound lessened.

"Good job," she whispered to the wolf as the wolf stood a few feet away, watching them.

Elizabeth slowly got up and backed away. Her work was done for now.

They exited the cave in silence, but everyone was alive with confidence and excitement.

"There haven't been wolf pups in well over two thousand years," Reis sounded hopeful.

"The pups of the Winter Wolf often will choose fae to defend, usually members of the royal family," Alant explained to Elizabeth, with a look to Janara.

"From the other seasons?" Elizabeth asked. Alant shook his head.

"No, usually from within their own court, unfortunately. There hasn't been any conflict with the other seasons for many years. The balance is too important to us all right now."

He stopped as Leonora came out of the trees near the gate.

"Knew it," she smirked, then before anyone could react, a wave of darkness took over Elizabeth. The last thing she heard was Alant yelling and Sable barking.

When Elizabeth awoke, she was back at the cabin in bed, Sable lying on her legs.

"Sable," Elizabeth coughed. Sable opened her eyes and crawled up to Elizabeth's chest, laying her head down and wagging her tail. Alant came into the cabin a while later, smiling when he saw she was awake.

"It's about time." He grinned, bringing her some water.

"What happened?" Elizabeth asked, sipping the water.

Alant sat down and started with when she'd been knocked out. Leonora had cast the spell at her. Janara had bound Leonora with a command, leaving Reis and Alant to take Elizabeth through the gate.

Sable had stayed with the young fae princess until they were through.

Then, Janara brought Sable to the gate. Alant had brought Elizabeth back and used what little skills he had.

"And a whole lot of hope," he added.

Alant, embarrassed, told Elizabeth how before Reis had been born, Leonora and he had been lovers and she'd never been able to let go of that.

Elizabeth was a threat because of how close their work and friendship kept them. Leonora hated her for that. What made it tricky was that Leonora was from a well-connected family, and Leonora had a seat on the Winter Council.

So when she'd seen the chance to legitimately get rid of Elizabeth for Janara and the dragon, she'd taken it.

Not only had Elizabeth defied orders to let a young fae royal into the realm, where she could be injured or taken by another season that didn't believe in balance, but Elizabeth had also gone against superstition.

That was enough for Leonora to convince the court that she needed to go.

"Well, that's a bit silly." Elizabeth sighed. She was a bit annoyed that he hadn't just told her all of this from the start. It was done though. She'd learned long ago that the past can't be different. She sat up to see Sable wriggling and hopping onto the floor.

"What about the wolf?" Elizabeth demanded, starting to get up.

"Stop," Alant put his hand on her, "She's fine, I gave Janara what she would need. Just rest, Leonora tried to kill you with that."

Later that day Alant went to the gateway and sent a message through for Reis.

Reis responded almost immediately that he would set up a meeting with the Wardens of Summer, Autumn, and Spring. It would be held the next morning at dawn, in a place between the gates of all the seasons.

For now, all they had to do was wait, so they went about their usual day.

They walked the island, Sable often bounding ahead of them through the snow, following small game tracks and sniffing under the trees. The sky was dark the next morning, with snow falling heavily around them as they made their way to the gate.

"Have I met these people before?" she asked ahead of him, ducking out of the way of a snow-laden branch.

"The other wardens?" he ducked beneath the branch. "Yes, I should expect so, unless there's been any that have retired."

"That will be strange, with me not knowing who they are."

He thought about it for a moment. "Honestly, I imagine that they all know, or at least have heard of it."

She frowned, feeling a gnawing sort of queasiness at the idea that this fae would know her when she didn't recall them, or even remember or know what it was to be fae.

Once they got to the gate, she told Sable to sit, and wait.

Alant said something under his breath, a language that her brain tried to make sense of but couldn't quite grasp.

The door opened, but instead of seeing the city that she had seen before, there was a swirling peach light.

Elizabeth and Alant stepped into it together. She felt a warm tingle wrap around her body, the smell of freshly falling leaves, the sound of trees in the wind, and the taste of strawberries on her tongue.

They were in a softly lit hall, with tall arched windows lining the walls. Outside each one, a different stage of the four seasons.

There was a large lounge area, with plush chairs surrounding an oval coffee table. Two women sat in chairs already, there was something ageless about them.

"They're of Summer," Alant informed her as they approached.

Elizabeth shook hands with each of them, she introduced herself, even though they knew who she was, while Alant caught up with them and made chit-chat.

"It is good to see you again, I am Cosma, and this is my sister, Sindri."

"I'm afraid I don't remember having met before," Elizabeth admitted.

"We heard you had been exiled. Your memories haven't returned?" Sindri asked, studying her. Elizabeth glanced at Alant.

"No, they haven't,"

Next the Autumn wardens, two men who looked as though they were twins and had the same ageless quality about them arrived.

She was greeted warmly but without much interest. The two Autumn Wardens were more concerned with talking to Alant about what had come through the winter gate.

They were quickly followed by the Spring wardens, two people that presented themselves as neither man nor woman. Instead, they seemed to exist somewhere within the sphere of both. They approached her and Alant.

"I'm Ensley, and this is my counterpart, Vesper. Wardens of Spring,"

"Nice to meet you."

"You as well," Vesper turned to Alant, "Good to see you again, Winter."

Alant smiled.

"And you Vesper," he turned to Elizabeth, "Sometimes, closer to the springtime, fae creatures from Winter or Spring will come into the mortal realm and end up going through the wrong gate."

"We end up working together more than you would expect," Ensley commented.

Just then Reis arrived. He was dressed more finely than Elizabeth had previously seen him.

He started to speak, "Wardens, I have heard from all of you. The balance is being restored in each of the season's realms. This is thanks to Elizabeth. Years ago, she was taken before the court then and her fate was decided."

"But this is a warden matter, so I put it to you, the wardens, to determine whether Elizabeth should remain in exile, or if she should be re-instated as a Warden," Reis continued.

Reis added, "She has healed the Winter Wolf, despite her exile. I wanted to ask your opinion before taking the matter to the Winter Court for a final, official decision. I will leave you to discuss"

Reis turned to Elizabeth, "Elizabeth, we will wait outside in the meantime."

# Chapter 8 Discussion Questions

1. Have you ever fainted?

_____________________________________

2. Have you ever confessed something to someone?

_____________________________________

_____________________________________

_____________________________________

3. Do you have favorite herbs? What ones do you like the scent of? What ones do you like the taste of? What ones do you like the look of?

_____________________________________

_____________________________________

_____________________________________

_____________________________________

_____________________________________

# Chapter 9

Reis led the way through a small iron door that she had not noticed before.

When they left the hall, they were in a small seating area. Elizabeth took a seat. How long would this take?

"Do you have an outcome that you hope for?" Reis asked as he sat in the chair next to her.

"Honestly, I don't know," and she didn't. On the one hand, she had felt something the past few days. An engagement that she hadn't experienced before, especially working with the creatures. But she also missed her home and her little routine. She wanted to get back to that.

"I suppose it isn't up to me though, is it?" She smiled, "Should I remain in exile, I will just continue as I have been. I do miss my home. But, if I'm reinstated, I'll get to keep helping fae creatures, and it seems like I'm rather good at it. I like that. I must have trained and practiced for several years."

"Well, you know where Janara and I stand," Reis smiled.

"Thank you. How is the wolf, by the way? Is she all right?"

"Janara did what you told her, and the light is getting darker each day. Winter is in a debt to you, Elizabeth, and that's what I'm telling the court."

It wasn't much longer before Alant came out, telling them it had been decided.

Chapter 9 Discussion Questions

1. If you were part of the fae, what seasonal court would you want to be a part of?

_______________________________________

2. What are some of your favorite things about each season?

_______________________________________

_______________________________________

_______________________________________

_______________________________________

_______________________________________

3. If you were Elizabeth would you want to be reinstated as a warden?

_______________________________________

_______________________________________

# Chapter 10

The waves were choppy but small. Elizabeth threw her weight into pushing her small boat into the water alongside Alant. She was going home.

They'd spent the past few days repairing the boat, mostly together but with some help from Reis as well.

"Come on Sable, load up," she told her, Sable, always eager for a boat ride, scrambled in.

Elizabeth hugged Alant, "Alright," She breathed, breaking the hug.

"I'll see you in a few weeks," she reminded herself.

"See you in a few weeks, be safe," Alant smiled.

Elizabeth got into the boat, started the small motor, and headed for home.

The wardens had decided that Elizabeth should be restored as a warden, and the court, mostly thanks to Janara and Reis, had agreed that she would be on a probationary period.

When she and Alant had returned to the cabin, she'd decided that she would split her time between the island and her home.

Elizabeth pat Sable as they navigated the waters, and as they passed by a sharp cliff, she looked up and saw a large silver wolf, with four small pups with bright shiny silver fur glistening in the sun.

# Chapter 10 Discussion Questions

1. Did you expect to see the wolf pups?

_______________________________________

2. What would be some good names for the wolf pups?

_______________________________________

_______________________________________

_______________________________________

_______________________________________

Erica Leduc lives in Hamilton, Ontario, with two cats, Dean and Dagney, and a dog, Hex. Between working to support them-self and spoil their pets, Erica likes practicing painting, exploring outdoors, and spending time focusing on bettering their communications and writing skills.

After years of working in food service and hospitality Erica Leduc wrote their first book, The Winter Wardens. This story was inspired by and written for people experiencing a decline in cognitive memory function.